P9-DYO-741

Date: 1/26/12

E SIMINOVICH
Siminovich, Lorena.
Alex and Lulu : two of a kind /

PALM BEACH COUNTY
LIBRARY SYSTEM
3650 Summit Boulevard
West Palm Beach, FL 33406-4198

To Alex, for being so refreshingly different

Copyright © 2008 by Lorena Siminovich

All rights reserved. No part of this book may be reproduced,
transmitted, or stored in an information retrieval system in any form
or by any means, graphic, electronic, or mechanical, including
photocopying, taping, and recording, without prior written
permission from the publisher.

First U.S. edition 2009

Library of Congress Cataloging-in-Publication Data is available.
Library of Congress Catalog Card Number 2008935206
ISBN 978-0-7636-4423-9

10 9 8 7 6 5 4 3 2 1

Printed in China

This book was typeset in Johann Light.

Edited by Libby Hamilton
Designed by Mike Jolley

A TEMPLAR BOOK

an imprint of
Candlewick Press
99 Dover Street
Somerville, Massachusetts 02144
www.candlewick.com

Alex and Lulu

Two of a Kind

Lorena Siminovich

templar books
an imprint of Candlewick Press

Alex and Lulu
are best friends.

They love to stop on their
way home from school
and play in the park.

On sunny days,
they just can't get enough
running, jumping, and
swinging!

Alex also likes to climb trees.
He hangs from the highest branches and calls,
"Lulu, look at me! There's no tree too high
for Alex the Incredible!"

But today Lulu is busy. She is watching the ants very closely,
because she is going to go home and paint a picture of them.
One day she is sure she will be a famous painter.

When big fat raindrops start to fall,
it's time to go home.

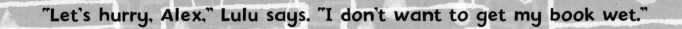

"Let's hurry, Alex," Lulu says. "I don't want to get my book wet."

But Alex doesn't want to hurry. And he doesn't want to stay dry.
He wants to jump in every single puddle.

"Alex," says Lulu, "we are just **SO** different."

"We are?" says Alex.

That night Alex and Lulu have a sleepover.
Lulu stays up late reading her book.

Alex stays awake too.
He is **thinking**.

Alex thinks about how much he likes soccer.
Every day, he is going to practice his shooting,

doing headers, and trapping the ball.

One day he will be
the Best Soccer Player in the World!

Then Alex remembers that Lulu doesn't like soccer.
It squashes her flowers and scares away the birds.

Next Alex remembers how, that afternoon,
he wanted to play a game of pretend.
He wanted to be the captain of a boat,
bound for adventures on the High Seas . . .

but Lulu wasn't interested.
She wanted to play at being
a famous artist who painted
huge pictures.

Alex is thinking very hard.
He goes to hide under a chair in the kitchen.

What if he and Lulu are
too **different** to be friends?

Just then Lulu opens the door.
"Found you!" she says.

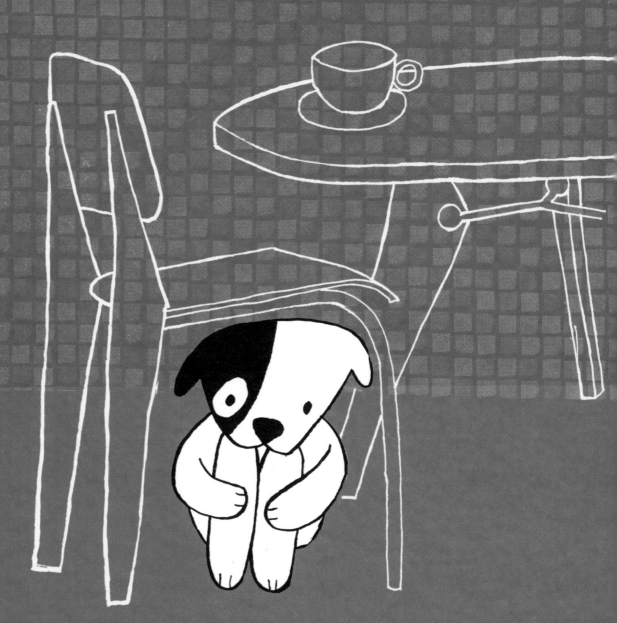

"Lulu," says Alex, who can't hold in his worry anymore,
"are we **opposites?**"

"I don't think so, Alex," says Lulu.
"Opposites are things like . . ."

big and small,

open and closed . . .

low and **high,**

wet and **dry,**

slow . . .

and fast.

"But you said it today—we are **SO** different from each other!" says Alex.

"I know," says Lulu. "But different is OK. It doesn't matter how different
we are when you think about all the things we like doing **together.**"

"You mean like playing on
the swings?" says Alex.
"Yes!" says Lulu. "And more—
I like reading and you like soccer,
but we both like . . . pillow fights!"

"And I like sailing on the High Seas," says Alex,
"but you like being a famous artist, so . . . you can paint our boat!"

"It's a deal," says Lulu. "Sometimes it's **because** we're so different
that we have the most fun when we're—"

"Together!" shouts Alex.

And it's true.
Alex and Lulu
are best friends.